CHICKEN
LITTLE
and THE BIG BAD WOLF

I AM SO **NOT** SCARED OF ANY WOLF!

SAM WEDELICH

SCHOLASTIC PRESS • NEW YORK

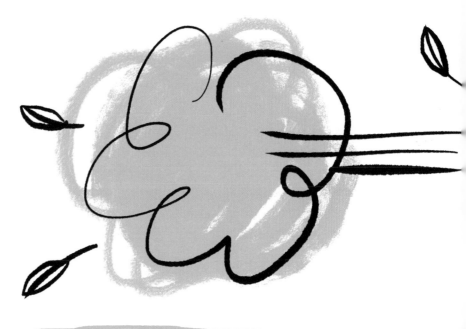

OH-NO
OH-NO
OH-
NO!

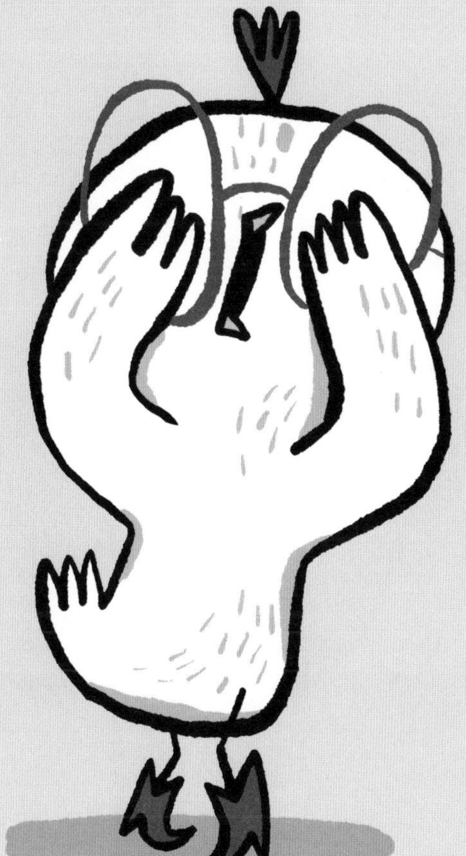

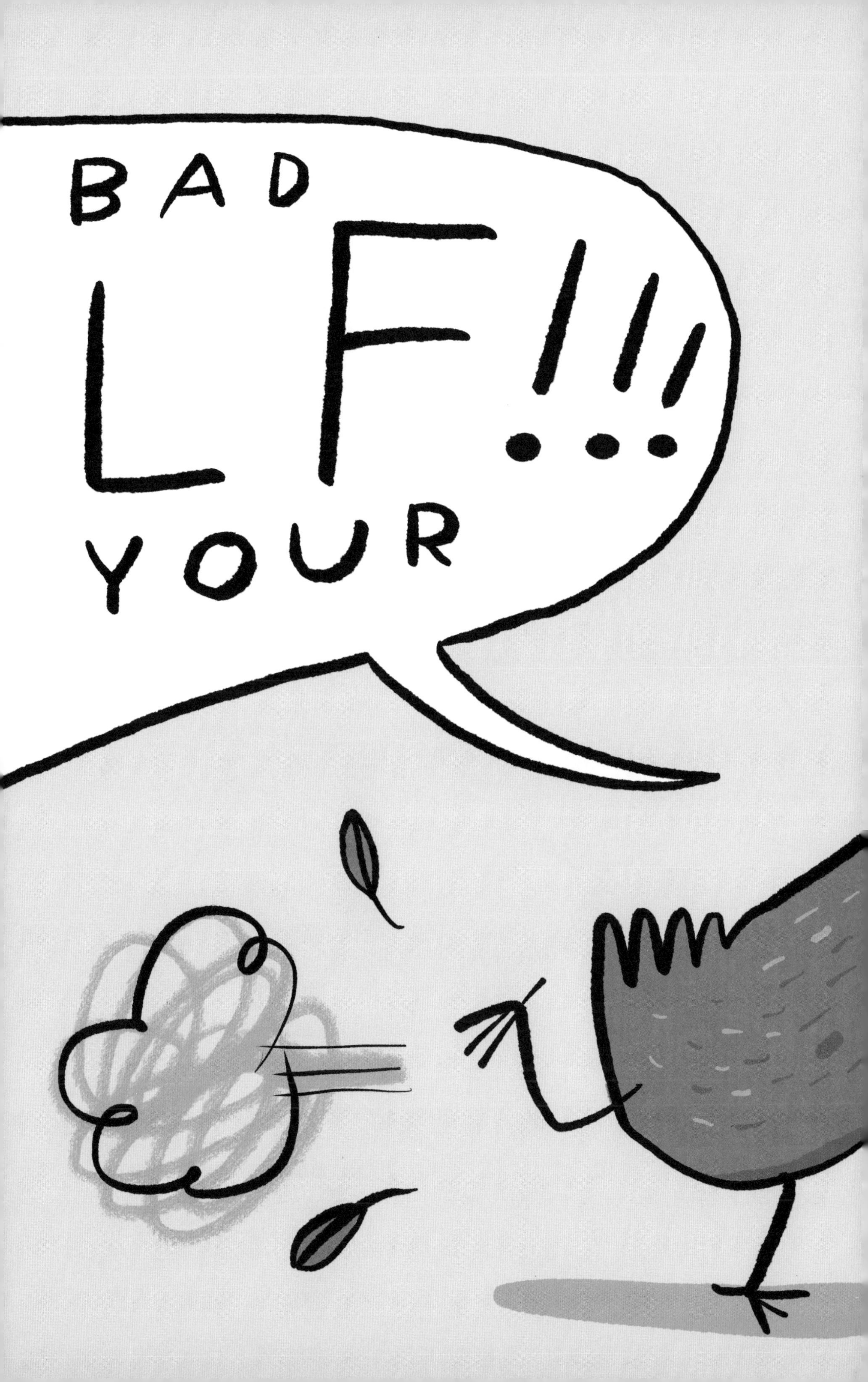
BAD LF!!! ... YOUR

RIDICULOUS! NO ONE CAN BEAT THE BIG BAD WOLF! WE NEED TO ESCAPE!
TEAM FLIGHT

THEY DIDN'T AGREE ON MUCH,
EXCEPT THAT HATCHING A PLAN WAS
MUCH HARDER THAN HATCHING EGGS!

ULTIMATELY, THEY DECIDED THEIR BEST OPTION WAS TO FLY THE COOP.

(BUT EVERYONE KNOWS CHICKENS AREN'T VERY GOOD AT FLYING!)

AND THEY WERE.

For anyone who's had to look for a place to belong . . .
and for all the flocks that welcomed them in.

• Library of Congress Cataloging-in-Publication Data available •
ISBN 978-1-338-35900-8 • 10 9 8 7 6 5 4 3 2 1   21 22 23 24 25 • Printed in China   62 • First edition, January 2021
Sam Wedelich's illustrations were created digitally. • The type was hand lettered by Sam Wedelich. • The set type is Amatic Regular. The book was printed on 120gsm woodfree and bound at Leo Paper. • Production was overseen by Catherine Weening. • Manufacturing was supervised by Shannon Rice. • The book was art directed and designed by Marijka Kostiw and edited by Tracy Mack.